Rabbit Blue

Written
and illustrated by
Marie-Louise Gay

Fitzhenry & Whiteside

First published in paperback by Fitzhenry and Whiteside in 2005

First published by Stoddart Kids in 1993

Published in Canada by Fitzhenry & Whiteside, 195 Allstate Parkway, Markham, Ontario L3R 4T8

Published in the United States by Fitzhenry & Whiteside, 121 Harvard Avenue, Suite 2, Allston, Massachusetts 02134

www.fitzhenry.ca   godwit@fitzhenry.ca

10 9 8 7 6 5 4 3 2 1

National Library of Canada Cataloguing in Publication

Gay, Marie-Louise
          Rabbit blue / written and illustrated by Marie-Louise Gay.

ISBN 1-55005-083-4

          I. Title.

PS8563.A868R23 2004   jC813'.54   C2003-903029-6

U.S. Publisher Cataloging-in-Publication Data
(Library of Congress Standards)

Gay, Marie-Louise.
    Rabbit Blue / Marie-Louise Gay. —1st ed.
[32] p. : col. ill. ; cm.
Previously published: Toronto: Stoddart Kids, 1993.
Summary: An energetic little girl with flyaway hair swings madly and sings about the amazing capabilities of her Rabbit Blue.
ISBN 1-55005-083-4 (pbk.)
1. Rabbits_ Fiction.   2. Imagination _ Fiction.   3. Play – Fiction.   I. Title.
  [E] 21   AC   PZ7.G39Ra 2003

Fitzhenry & Whiteside acknowledges with thanks the Canada Council for the Arts, the Government of Canada through the Book Publishing Industry Development Program (BPIDP), and the Ontario Arts Council for their support of our publishing program.

Printed in Hong Kong.

To my rabbit heroes, Peter, Bugs, and Janet of the Bunny Planet

Let me tell you
a thing or two
about my friend
Rabbit Blue...

Rabbit Blue loves to fly

through fog and rain

and purple sky.

Rabbit Blue

swings round and round

high and low

and upside down.

Rabbit Blue loves to swim.

There he is!

Look at him!

Rabbit Blue

can catch a ball,

a planet or a star

about to fall.

Rabbit Blue feels yellow heat

and hears the thud

of the jungle beat.

Rabbit Blue

twirls his ears

and in a flash

he disappears...

But if you're awake around half past two
you're sure to see my Rabbit Blue.